3

1893

FOR BREAD

Mary Z. Holmes
Illustrated by Geri Strigenz

STONE
BANK
BOOKS

RAINTREE
STECK-VAUGHN
LIBRARY
Austin, Texas

For Darby

This text and art were reviewed for accuracy by Dr. William Falkowski, author of a dissertation entitled: "Accommodation and Conflict: Patterns of Polish Immigrant Adaptation to Industrial Capitalism and American Political Pluralism in Buffalo, New York, 1873-1901," State Univeristy of New York, Buffalo, NY.

Designed by Geri Strigenz

Published by Raintree/Steck-Vaughn Library
P.O. Box 26015, Austin, TX 78755

Library of Congress Cataloging-in-Publication Data
Holmes, Mary Z.
    For bread / Mary Z. Holmes ; illustrated by Geri Strigenz.
        p. cm. — (History's children)
    "A Stone Bank Book"
    Summary: In 1893 in Buffalo, New York, thirteen-year-old Stefan helps his financially troubled Polish American family survive hard times by making and selling drawings.
        ISBN 0-8114-3501-6. — ISBN 0-8114-6426-1 (pbk.)
        1. Polish Americans—Juvenile fiction. [1. Polish Americans—Fiction. 2. Artists—Fiction. 3. Buffalo (N.Y.)—Fiction.] I. Strigenz, Geri K., ill. II. Title. III. Series: Holmes, Mary Z. History's children.
PZ7.H7375Fo 1992   91-37279
[Fic]—dc20   CIP AC

Printed in the United States of America
1 2 3 4 5 6 7 8 9 WZ 96 95 94 93 92

1893

This story takes place in the city of Buffalo, New York, at the eastern end of Lake Erie. In 1893, over 250,000 people live here. Times are hard in this large port and railway center. Many people are out of work.

More than 50,000 Poles live on Buffalo's east side. They have come to America from Poland in search of good jobs and a better life. They speak Polish and have built their own churches and schools. The Poles are hard working, but the year is going badly for them. Hundreds of men have no jobs.

Polish Glossary

Mamusia	*(mah-MOO-shah)* Mama
Tata	*(TAH-tah)* Papa
babuszka	*(bah-BOOSH-kah)* a head scarf
za chlebem	*(zah-HLEB-em)* for bread, *meaning* to make a better living

Note

In Stefan's story, his family and the people in his community speak Polish. As you read, imagine that Stefan is telling you the story in the Polish language.

When characters in this book speak English, the words they say will be printed in italic type like this: *"I don't understand Polish,"* he said. Polish-speaking people just learning to speak English may say *dat* for the word *that*, *vun* for *one*, and *ve* for *we*.

Historical Personages

The following people mentioned in this book really lived in Buffalo in 1893:

Father Jan Pitass
Jumbo Sroka

I

THE ARTIST

I finished the mathematics lesson and drew a small house at the bottom of the page. Feliks bumped me with his elbow just as I did the roof and chimney. I gave him a jab in the ribs. Our schoolroom was so crowded that three of us shared each desk. I sat at the left end of the bench. My friend, Feliks, sat in the middle, and Zygmunt was on the right. When I jabbed Feliks, he pushed Zygmunt, who slid off the bench to the floor.

"Stefan Nowicki!" Mr. Glinski yelled. I jumped to my feet.

"Yes, sir," I said.

"Do we have you to thank for Zygmunt's fall?" he asked.

"Yes, sir. I'm sorry. We're too crowded."

Glinski sighed and looked up at the ceiling. "God is punishing us all," he said. "For me, the punishment is having to teach thirteen-year-old Polish boys who cannot sit still."

We all laughed. Glinski was an excellent teacher and a good man. He walked over to me and put his hand out for my mathematics lesson. "More houses, Stefan?" he asked, looking over the work. "Yes, yes, yes. The numbers are correct. Good."

Glinski scratched his head and looked out the window. I sat down with relief. I always drew buildings on my schoolwork. It was because I didn't have my own paper to draw on at home. So far, my teacher didn't seem to mind.

When the bell rang, we left the classroom in as orderly a fashion as sixty wild boys could. Children streamed out the front door of the school into a cold blast of February air. They ran in all directions. Feliks and I caught up with my sister, Fabianna, and my brother, Leon. They were younger. Fabianna was twelve, Leon ten.

We gasped at the cold. The temperature had been around zero for over a week. The packed snow squeaked under our feet as we rushed home. Feliks told Fabianna how we had pushed Zygmunt off the bench. She laughed, and a puff of steam blew from her mouth. We darted across the street in front of horses pulling a beer wagon. Whatever the driver yelled at us, his words were blown away by the wind.

"He had nothing nice to say anyway," Leon said. I pulled his cap down over his eyes.

When we reached our street, I saw a well-dressed man standing across from our house. He seemed to be writing. I was curious.

"Go ahead," I told the others. "I'll be right in."

As I came closer to the man, I saw that he was drawing the row of houses across the street.

"That's my house you're drawing," I said.

He looked up and said. *"I don't understand Polish."*

I switched to English. *"Is my house you draw."*

"Oh, really. Which one?" he asked, showing me the drawing.

"Dat vun." I pointed it out. *"Vhy you draw dese houses?"*

"I work for the newspaper. It's writing a story about the Poles. I'm drawing pictures to go with the story." The man tucked his cold hands under his armpits for a moment. He shifted from foot to foot in the cold.

"Vhich paper it is?" I asked.

"Express," he told me, as he started to draw again. The *Express* was an important newspaper in Buffalo. It was written for the English-speaking people.

I watched as he drew a garbage barrel in the picture. Then he sketched a woman and a child. I thought he did well, especially the

6

drawings of people. *"Is good,"* I said. Buildings I could draw, but not people. Maybe he could tell me how to improve my work, I thought.

"Watch next week's papers for the story," he said. Then, before I could tell him about my own drawing, the man rushed off. *"See you, kid,"* he called over his shoulder.

I ran across the rutted, icy street and through the narrow walkway between houses. Wait until I tell my mother, I thought. I had talked to a real artist.

"Mamusia," I called to her as I opened the back door.

"Stefan, hurry in and close the door," she said. When I came into the kitchen, she looked up at me. "From the look on your face, you have something to say. But let it wait until later."

The younger children swarmed around her as Mamusia stirred the soup pot. There was baby Katarzyna, who was one year old. She was crying and hanging on to Mamusia's skirt. Poor little thing had a cold. Three-year-old Tadeusz sat on the floor at Mamusia's feet. Zuzanna was struggling to put on two sweaters and mittens. She was five. Fabianna bent down to help. She tied a babuszka on Zuzanna's head and wrapped a shawl around her.

Leon came into the kitchen with old cloth sacks. "We're going out for wood before dark," he said. He handed out the sacks and tied his scarf tighter around his neck.

"Watch Zuzanna," Mamusia called as we left. "Keep her off the railway tracks."

"Where's Feliks?" I asked Fabianna, leading the way.

"At the tracks," she said. "He said to meet him there."

We took a shortcut between some houses and came out at the next street. Other children were headed for the railway yards to look for wood too. Leon, Zuzanna, Fabianna, and I began to run. When Zuzanna slid and fell on a patch of ice, I pulled her to her feet. "Are you hurt?" I asked, brushing her off. She just smiled and started running again.

Firewood was needed for our stoves. Children, who couldn't earn money with jobs, could save money for the family by finding wood and bringing it home. This was important in the cold

Buffalo winter. A good place to look was at the busy railway yards. Buffalo was a port on Lake Erie. Here, goods from the Midwest came on lake barges and were put on trains for shipment east. Train cars were built here, and there was wood from broken crates and barrels lying about. Sometimes lumber fell off the trains. If you knew where to look, there were wood scraps to be found.

"Stefan, over here," Feliks called, as we reached the yards. He made his way over several sets of tracks to meet us. "Something's happening over at the sidetracks. Come on."

"Train coming," someone yelled, and we all stepped back. Fabianna looked around quickly for Zuzanna and grabbed her hand. Many people had been killed by the trains.

"This way." Feliks pointed and took off. We ran alongside the moving train. Other children waited for it to pass, but we didn't want to waste time.

Then we heard a gunshot and men yelling. The police were chasing a man away from some boxcars sitting on a sidetrack. Instead of following the chase to see what would happen, we ran to the sidetrack. The man had probably been breaking into a boxcar to steal whatever was inside.

Leon spotted the car first. "Look at this," he cried. The man had pried off three large boards. You could see into the boxcar, but that did not interest us. The wood was the prize.

Feliks and Leon held a board up on one end. Fabianna and I jumped on it to break it into smaller pieces. Finally, the boards were broken, and we stuffed the wood into our sacks.

"My fingers are freezing," Leon said. "My feet too." He threw his sack over his shoulder. "I want to go home."

"Yes, we must leave," I said. "The police will be coming back to the car. Is everyone ready?"

"Oh, no," I heard Fabianna gasp. "Where is Zuzanna?" She was nowhere in sight.

"Holy Mother," I prayed, looking around. Fabianna was already running along the parked boxcars, calling for our sister. Leon and Feliks went in the other direction. I looked inside the boxcar to see if Zuzanna had crawled in. Then I fell to the icy

ground and looked under it.

She was huddled beneath the boxcar, her shawl caught on something. "Help me, Stefan," she said. I gave her a pull and dragged her out. She got to her feet and lifted the sack. "There was coal under there," she said with a grin. "I got it."

"Do you know how dangerous that is?" I shouted at her. "What if the train started moving?"

A tear slid down her cheek, and Zuzanna wiped it off with her mitten. A smudge of coal dust streaked her face. I patted her on the head and picked up her sack.

"So much coal, little sister." I gave her a wink. "I'll carry it for you."

I called the others, and we hurried away from the boxcars.

It was getting dark. The wind felt even colder. Walking back to our block, we huddled close together. Soon the streets were full of men in their dark clothes, making their way home from work.

"There's Tata," Leon said and called out to our father.

Tata was just ahead. He looked tired, but he smiled as we caught up. "So much wood tonight," he said. "What a good job."

"And coal too," Zuzanna said, grabbing Tata's hand.

"I saw an artist today," I blurted out.

Tata shook his head. "More foolishness, Stefan?" He didn't want me to fill my head with fancy ideas about drawing. Tata always said I must get a good job and work hard when I finished school. Maybe at the railway yards where he worked.

I shivered. Even the inside of my nose was freezing.

11

II

THE NEWSPAPER

As we ate our supper that same night, Fabianna gave me a chance to tell about the artist.

"Who was that man on the street?" she asked.

"He works for the *Express*." I swallowed a spoonful of soup. "He was drawing the houses on the block. Ours too. The paper is doing a story about the Poles."

"The *Express* is writing about our people?" Tata asked.

"That's what he told me. For next week's papers."

Mamusia jiggled Katarzyna on her knee as she ate. "Our house is going to be in the paper?" she asked. "Tadeusz, wipe your face."

I nodded. Tadeusz rubbed his face on his sleeve.

"I'll ask at the saloon," Tata said. "Maybe Binkowski knows about this." The news would soon spread throughout the neighborhood. All the men stopped at Binkowski's saloon to find out what was going on. "He can get a paper for us. Would you like that?" he asked my mother.

"We can cut the picture out," Mamusia said. "We could send it to the family in Poland. Imagine having a picture of our house."

"But, Mamusia," I said, "I can draw you a picture anytime."

Tata gave me a dark look and pushed his chair from the table. He would go to Binkowski's now and tell the men.

"Get the rent before you go," Mamusia said. "And bring home

12

the money." She was in charge of the money in our family. There were two special jars on the shelf in the pantry. Mamusia put money for the house payment in one. In the other was church and food money. She probably kept another jar hidden.

"Yes, yes," Tata said. He threw on his jacket and left by the back door. Our house had eight rooms. We lived in the four small rooms at the back. Tata rented out the two rooms at the front to the Mielecki family. They had six children, just as we did. The two middle rooms were rented to the Nowaks, who had only two babies. I could hear Tata knocking on the side door in the walkway now. Each family would pay him $2.50 for the month's rent.

We did not expect Tata back so soon, but he poked his head in the back door and gave Mamusia the money.

"Bad news," he said. "Nowak lost his job. I'm going to the saloon with him. Maybe Binkowski knows of some work."

When Tata had gone, Mamusia put Katarzyna in the cradle and sat down to patch a shirt. Fabianna cleaned off the table. Leon took Tadeusz and Zuzanna to the outhouse in the back yard. I went out to the shed to check on the ducks. I poured a scoop of feed into the trough for them. The ducks had buried themselves in the straw, trying to keep warm. There were no eggs to bring in.

Why was drawing all right for the artist, but not for me, I wondered.

The newspaper story was printed the next week. What an uproar it caused! Tata brought home a paper and tossed it on the table. He told Fabianna to translate the story for us. She was the best with English.

As she spread the paper out, I looked at the drawings that were printed with the story. Our street was there, and the artist had drawn another picture of a woman. She wore rags. The walls of her dirty kitchen were full of holes. What was this?

Fabianna translated the story from English to Polish as we listened. Tata's face wore a frown. Mamusia put her hand to her mouth in shock.

The story said the Poles were dirty and jabbered in another language. It said our houses smelled and were not clean. It called the men lazy and not smart enough to make work for themselves. The Poles went to the Buffalo Poormaster's office to get handouts like beggars, it said.

Tata slammed his hand on the table. "This is not true," he said. "We are not dirty, stupid people. I work hard. I saved money to buy this house, which your mother keeps clean. I don't beg money from the Poormaster."

"They laugh because we speak Polish?" Mamusia asked with amazement. "How can that be? It is our language."

"Burn this." Tata handed the paper to me. Before I threw the paper into the iron stove, I ripped the street drawing out and slipped it into my pocket. Tata was shouting, "How can they say such things?"

Everyone was talking about the newspaper story. Mr. Glinski talked about it in school. I heard about it when gathering wood. Each night, the men talked it over together.

Tata was still angry on Saturday. There had been a heavy snow, and the two of us were shoveling a path in the back yard.

"Za chlebem. For bread, Stefan," Tata said. "We came to this country for bread. To make a better living."

Tadeusz and Zuzanna were tumbling in the snow and laughing. I lifted a heavy load of snow and threw it to the side. I remembered coming to America. It was before Tadeusz, Zuzanna, and Katarzyna were born. That was six years ago.

Tata stopped to blow on his cold hands. "We rented a room when we came. Do you remember?"

"Yes, Tata," I said. Fabianna, Leon, Tata, Mamusia, and I had all lived in a single room. "Then you found a good job."

"Your mother took charge of my wages," Tata smiled. "I worked hard, and she pinched every penny. That we were able to buy this house is due to her." He shoveled snow off the path. Tadeusz squealed as the snow hit him.

"A man has to work. For bread," Tata said. "To feed his children. Good hard work."

By good hard work, Tata did not mean drawing, I thought. He meant a job at the railway yards or the factories. A real job that

brought money home to the family.

A snowball hit me in the back of my head. I turned around, and Zuzanna giggled. I packed a snowball and tossed it at her.

Tata ignored us. "The newspaper story lies," he said as he worked. There was a frown on his face again.

At Sunday Mass in St. Stanislaus church, Father Jan Pitass talked about the newspaper story. By now, everyone had heard about it.

"It is not true," Father Pitass said, shaking his head in sadness. "This newspaper article isn't fair. Some Polish men are out of work, that is so. But so are many other men in Buffalo. Times are very bad." He looked at all the people crowded into the church. "You don't look like dirty, stupid, lazy people to me. I'm proud of you for working so hard."

I sat in the pew with my brothers, sisters, and parents. We listened closely to what the priest was saying. When it was necessary, he fought for us. Father Pitass had seen to it that we had our own Polish churches and schools. Many families had gotten help from him. Sometimes he was tough, but he was a hero to us.

When the choir sang, I looked to find Feliks. He usually was a fine singer, but lately his voice was breaking. When he was talking, he would suddenly squeak. Now, I heard him sing off-key. Father Pitass heard it too and jumped to his feet.

Pointing at Feliks, Father Pitass shouted, "If you cannot do any better, stop. I do not want any meowing in my church." Feliks turned red and closed his mouth. Oh, yes, the priest could be tough at times.

Fabianna bowed her head. I could see her shoulders shaking. She was giggling. I pinched my lips together, as I tried not to laugh out loud. Feliks would be teased about this for weeks.

Later outside the church, Father Pitass was talking to the families. When he saw Feliks, he grabbed him by the ear. "Shame on you. Such singing," he said.

"I'm sorry, Father," Feliks said, and his voice cracked again. Fabianna and I grinned.

The priest patted him on the back. "You are a good boy," he

said. "Your voice will improve." Then he turned to talk to Mr. Nowak, our renter who was out of work. I heard them talking about Poland.

Feliks walked back to our block with us. His parents and mine talked about the newspaper story. Leon, Tadeusz, and Zuzanna climbed up the tall banks of snow and slid down. Fabianna carried baby Katarzyna on her hip and told Feliks not to worry.

"This is terrible," Feliks sighed. "Now everyone will make fun of me."

"No, they won't," Fabianna comforted him.

"Meow," Leon called at Feliks from the snowbank.

Feliks and I ran after Leon and rolled him in the snow. Zuzanna joined in too, jumping on Leon when he was down. "Children," Mamusia scolded.

Even with Feliks's shame in church and the upset over the newspaper story, I remember that day as a happy one. Then on Monday, when we came home from school, Tata was there.

"I've lost my job," he told us. "The bosses at the railway yards told us there was no more work."

We were frightened.

III

OUT OF WORK

Mamusia sat at the table with the money jars in front of her. "This we cannot touch," she said, pointing at the jar with the house payment money. "And sixty dollars more is needed for the payment due this summer." She put her hand on the other jar. "Food and church money, only enough for a week."

She pulled a babuszka from her pocket and untied it. Coins rolled out onto the table. "This was put aside for shoes. We must use it for food now."

"Here is what we will do," Tata said. "I'll find work. Maybe a new job or a week here and a week there. My boss at the train yards said he would hire me to shovel the tracks each time it snows. There will be other things to do. You are not to worry."

Zuzanna suddenly started to cry. Tata told her not to be afraid. "You must find work after school, Stefan. You'll have to use your head. Go to the shops and ask what you can do."

"Yes, Tata," I said, hoping to bring home a few pennies every day to put into the jar.

"Fabianna, find washing to do for our neighbors," Tata said. "But you'll have to do it alone. Mamusia is already busy."

"I can do it," Fabianna told him. This would be hard work — carrying water to heat on the stove, scrubbing clothes, and ironing.

Tata looked at Leon. "You and Zuzanna must bring home the wood by yourselves. You must keep her safe."

Zuzanna looked up at me and down again quickly. She was thinking about crawling under the train. Leon would have to watch her very carefully.

Leon said, "I will, Tata."

"Promise me you will not complain about food," Mamusia said. "I won't be buying any meat. And I'll save the two cents extra it costs to buy fresh bread."

We promised. Then Tata asked for God's blessing on our family.

The next day after school, I set out to earn money. Luck was with me. At the bakery, Mr. Wozniak had just come back from the market with three sacks of flour. They were unloaded from the horse cart behind the shop, but not yet carried inside.

"I'll pay you one penny for bringing the bags in," he said and went back into the bakery.

I stood in the snow and studied the sacks. They were very big. I had to get them up three wooden steps and inside the door. How heavy could they be?

I bent down to lift the first sack and found out. The sack must have weighed one hundred pounds. I couldn't even budge it. I gave the sack a kick and sat down on it. What would Tata say if I failed at my first job? I couldn't give up. I must do this for bread, as Tata would say. To take care of the family.

Since I couldn't lift, I'd have to somehow roll the sacks up the steps. I'd give it a try.

I pushed the first sack as hard as I could. My feet dug into the snow as I worked. Finally, it fell over against the first step. I pushed it to make it stand up on the step. Then I pushed until it fell against the second step. Again, I pushed it to make it stand up. Pushed until it fell over on the third step. Pushed and rolled it over and into the door. I was exhausted.

With trembling legs, I went down the steps for the second sack. When I got it standing up, it suddenly fell back and knocked me down. My leg was under its heavy weight.

20

"How are you doing?" Mr. Wozniak called from the door.

"Just fine." I managed a weak smile.

So, I started over with the second sack. After much struggle, it was inside the door with the first. Although it was cold outside, I was hot under my sweater. My arms ached.

Finally, the third sack was in the bakery. It had taken me nearly an hour. Wozniak gave me a penny. "Here's a loaf of bread for you too," he said. "You're a good worker."

"Thank you." A good worker! A man could have finished the job in five minutes, I thought. I must have been a funny sight fighting with the sacks of flour.

I walked home more tired than I had ever been. Mamusia smiled when I gave her the bread and dropped the penny in the jar.

I brought home a few pennies almost every day. Sometimes, there was no work to be found. But usually I picked up odd jobs to do for the shopkeepers. I scrubbed the floor in the butcher shop, swept up at Binkowski's saloon, and carried boxes of goods at the grocery. Wozniak liked me, so he saved the job of bringing in the flour sacks for me. Once a week, I wore myself out rolling them up his back steps. How I hated those flour sacks. The day after, I would fall asleep in school.

I missed the time I used to spend with Feliks. We still shared the same desk during the day, but we couldn't be together after school. He still had to get wood for his family. I knew he was keeping an eye on Leon and Zuzanna. He was a fine friend.

Tata couldn't find a full-time job. More and more men were out of work. As the weeks passed, there were more snowfalls. Then he returned to the railway yards to see his old boss and shovel the tracks. From time to time, he picked up a day of work at the docks, unloading the barges. Sometimes, he got a few days at a factory or slaughterhouse. Lines of worry appeared around his eyes, but he never stopped looking for work.

We managed as best we could. Mamusia fed us soup made from vegetables she had preserved from our own garden. She tried to be brave. I knew she was worried about saving the money needed for the house payment. It would be terrible to lose the

house.

One Saturday morning, Mamusia was outside emptying the ashes from the stove. When she came back in, she looked very upset.

"What is it?" Fabianna asked her.

"My God, my God," Mamusia cried. "Mrs. Nowak told me they're going back to Poland. Her husband cannot find a job, and her babies are sick. They want to go home."

"Sit down, Mamusia," said Fabianna, as she patted her arm.

"They're leaving tomorrow." Mamusia put her hands to her face. "We need that rent money." She started to cry. "This will upset your father, and he has too much to worry about."

This was something I could help with. "I'll find new renters," I said. "Please don't cry, Mamusia."

"You're a good boy, Stefan," she said, as she wiped her eyes. "Bless you, son."

I left the house right away and headed for Binkowski's saloon. He knew everything that went on in our neighborhood. He found jobs and rooms for people. For those who could not write, he wrote letters to their families in Poland. He also sold ship tickets for people who wanted to go back home. The Nowaks had probably bought their tickets from him.

Binkowski came outside to talk to me. The weather was warming, and the melting snow had turned the street to slush and mud. He wiped his fat face with his bar apron.

"Ah. Feels good. The sun," he said.

"Do you know anyone who needs two rooms?" I asked.

"No. No one." He hooked his thumbs in his suspenders. "Your best chance is to find someone at the train station."

"Thanks, Mr. Binkowski," I said and took off. I hopped the mud holes in the street and ran several blocks to the station. A train had just come in from New York.

People were getting off the train. I pushed through the crowd, watching for Polish families new to Buffalo. Three families I saw were met by other people. Their rooms were probably already arranged. Then I saw a family looking around, as if deciding what to do next. I would try them.

"Do you need a place to live?" I asked. "My father has two clean rooms for $2.50 a month."

"A nice Polish boy to welcome us to Buffalo," the man said and smiled. "I am Roman Witkowski, just arrived from Poland. This is my family."

"How do you do. I am Stefan Nowicki." I nodded my head to the man and his wife. One of their little girls giggled at me. "Do you need a place to live?" I asked again.

"So eager to do business," Mr. Witkowski laughed. "Perhaps we could come and look at the rooms first?"

I picked up some of their bundles. "Oh, yes. Just follow me." I led them out of the station and down the street. I was so proud. They followed me block after block — Mr. and Mrs. Witkowski and four trailing children.

Tata was home when we arrived. He showed Witkowski the two middle rooms, where the Nowaks were packing up. Witkowski said the rooms would do. Since the Nowaks were staying for one more night, the new family would sleep in our kitchen.

"Excellent, Stefan," Tata said. "You make me proud."

That night we sat in our crowded kitchen and heard about Poland. Tata brought in the Nowaks, and we gave them a going-away party. They brought dumplings, and Mrs. Witkowski took some sausages and cheese out of her bundle. Mamusia fixed it up in a fine feast. We sang songs and danced as best we could in the small room. Bad times were not all bad.

IV

TONAWANDA

After the snow season, Tata had trouble finding any work. Every night, he sat silently at the table. He would run his fingers through his hair and look up at the jar on the shelf. We needed to be putting more money in for the house payment. "I have to find work," he would say.

Then a man called Jumbo Sroka told the men about work at the Tonawanda docks, just a little to the north of Buffalo. Men needing work should come to the Broadway station. They would take the Belt Line railway up to Tonawanda and unload lumber from the barges. The pay was forty cents an hour. Mamusia was happy that good work was available.

"There's a catch," Tata said. "The work is there because the lumbershovers are on strike." The lumbershovers were dock-workers at Tonawanda. Their group had called a strike, and they had walked off the job. Now, the lumberyard owners wanted to hire Poles from Buffalo to work in the strikers' places.

"That would make me a scab," said Tata.

"What's that?" Leon asked. I already knew what a scab was.

"A scab takes a striker's job," Tata explained. "The strikers hate the scabs for taking their work. It will be dangerous. The strikers may try to beat us up."

"Don't do it," Mamusia said. "Somehow, we will manage."

25

Tata shook his head. "I haven't found work for a week," he said. "I'll go to Tonawanda. I must bring home money."

So early every morning, Tata went down to the Broadway station, where there was pushing and shoving to get a day's job in Tonawanda. Each day, Jumbo Sroka picked three hundred men to go on the train. Tata was lucky. He was big and strong, and he was always hired.

It was dangerous. We heard of men being attacked by the strikers. A sheriff and eleven deputies were hired to protect our men — the scabs who took the strikers' jobs.

One night, Tata was late coming home from the train station. Mamusia worried and worried. Then she could not bear it any longer. "Go out and find him," she finally said.

Fabianna and I had gone only a few blocks from home when we found him. He was hanging onto a lamppost. Blood ran down his face from a cut in his forehead.

"Oh, Tata," Fabianna cried.

"Help me home, children," Tata said. "I'm too dizzy to do it on my own."

I ducked under Tata's arm and let him lean on me. "What happened to you?" I asked. "Was it the strikers?" Fabianna supported his other side.

"I was running to catch the return train," Tata told us. "A group of strikers started to throw rocks. Then they attacked us with sticks. Somehow we made it to the train."

"Oh, Tata." Fabianna began to cry. "Please don't go back."

Tata stumbled against me heavily, and we almost fell over. Slowly, he pulled himself up, and we walked on.

"For bread," he said tiredly. "You understand, Stefan."

I did understand. Tata would go through anything to take care of our family, even if it hurt him. He'll go back, I thought.

As we brought Tata to the house, he said, "I won't give up."

That May, it was hard for me to pay attention in class. Instead of drawing houses, I drew shops on my schoolwork. The grocery, the carpenter shop, and the funeral parlor reminded me of where I would look for work after school. And I drew trains.

Glinski, my teacher, said my schoolwork was suffering, but my drawing was better than ever. Foolishness, I thought. I had been stupid to think I could be an artist when I grew up. Hard work, even dangerous work, was required of a man.

When June came and school was over, I had all day to find work. Feliks and I worked as partners then. I even let him take the bakery job one week. What a laugh I had watching him fight the flour sacks up the bakery steps. Never again, he told me. We found odd jobs at the Broadway market. The butchers, bakers, and farmers selling their goods had need of boys to run errands for them. On a good day, I brought home as much as fifteen cents for the money jar.

Then Tata came rushing home one night with news about Tonawanda. "We walked off the job," he told us. "The Polish workers are on strike now."

"The scabs are on strike?" I asked. How could this be?

"The owners were paying forty cents an hour. Today they say they will pay for the number of boards we unload," Tata said, trying to catch his breath. He was excited. "It's their way of tricking us. With the new way, we'll earn only twenty-five cents an hour."

Mamusia shook her head. "They weren't fair to you."

"We walked off the job together," Tata said. "Tomorrow we're going back to get our pay. I want Stefan to come along. He should see how Poles can stick together." He looked at me. Of course, I wanted to go along!

"Not if it's dangerous," Mamusia told him.

"The strikers won't hurt us now. They even gave us a party today," Tata laughed. "The Poles are strikers too."

The next day, Tata and I caught the Belt Line train to Tonawanda. One hundred other strikers came along. We sang Polish songs, and the men cheered themselves for uniting against the owners. We noticed that there were some other men who weren't celebrating. These Poles were intending to work as scabs today.

A fight broke out on the train. Tata and the striking men told the others to join with them against the owners.

28

"The owners tricked us," a man told the others. "They'll trick you too. Yesterday we worked for forty cents an hour. Today you work for twenty-five cents. Tomorrow, maybe fifteen."

"You cannot trust the owners," Tata told them. "Join the strike with us."

The men who wanted to work had the same look that I had seen before on Tata's face. They wouldn't listen. They needed the jobs and the money.

"Scabs!" a man shouted. "Poles should stick together." He made a fist and swung at another man.

"Stay close to me, Stefan," Tata said, as he pulled me away from the fight. "There may be trouble after all." He took me to the end of the car. I looked out the window at the stormy sky.

"I don't understand, Tata," I said loudly over the noise of the men. "Before you worked as a scab. And now you fight the scabs."

"I made a decision to work as a scab. As one man," he told me. "Now we decide as a group. Poles together are stronger against the owners."

"But you still need a job."

"Yes," he nodded. "Sometimes, you have to take risks."

I was still confused about the strike. What Tata said made sense in a way. The Poles should work together. But what if it meant no work? I thought about the money jar at home. I was scared.

When the train approached Tonawanda from the south, our men forced the train driver to stop at the offices of the owners. They pulled the scabs off the train. "We won't let you work today," our group told them.

Tata said to hurry, and we joined our group of strikers gathered at the front of the offices. Thunder rumbled in the distance. What would happen now, I wondered.

"Vhere is the president?" one man called out in English. *"Vhere is the president?"* Other men took up the call.

The president of the owner's group came out the door. With him were the sheriff and his deputies. They had guns.

"Give us our pay," someone yelled.

"You'll be paid for the hours you worked," said the president. *"The paymaster first has to check his accounts."* Nobody believed him.

Tata yelled, *"You have money in safe. Give it to us!"*

I looked around at the other Poles, who repeated his words. *"Give it to us!"* they shouted. The crowd moved closer to the door. I was pushed along with it.

The sheriff held up his gun. *"The first man who attempts to cross the threshold of this door will die on the spot,"* he shouted over the noise of the crowd. The sky grew darker.

One striker cried, *"Ve got to die but once. Ve might as vell do it now."* Someone threw a rock at the sheriff. Then rocks hit the front of the building. The president hurried back inside. As more rocks sailed through the air, the sheriff and his deputies ducked back in too.

The crowd was angry now. *"Again you trick us!"* Someone took a wooden match out of his pocket and lit it. Holding the match above his head, he shouted to those in the building. *"Ve vill burn dis lumberyard."* More men lit matches and echoed, *"Burn the lumberyard."*

With a loud crack of thunder, the rain suddenly started to pour down on us. I pulled my jacket up around my neck. The rain put out the matches and soaked our clothes. Water streamed off the end of Tata's nose.

"This will cool us down," he said.

"What will happen next?" I asked.

"Somehow we'll get the pay that's coming to us."

The men backed away from the building and formed into small groups. Later, when the rain stopped, I took off my jacket to wring it out. Tata was busy talking. Leaving him, I followed a rut in the road that was filled with rainwater. A leaf floated in it. I wondered what the men would do next.

A man stepped in front of me. I looked up. It was a National Guard soldier, pointing a rifle at me. At the end of the rifle was a bayonet, inches from my chest.

"Go back to the group, boy," he ordered me.

For a few seconds I could not move. Then I turned and ran back to my father. "Tata," I cried, pulling on his wet jacket. "The soldiers are here." The soldiers marched up with their rifles ready. A few rocks were thrown at them, but the crowd waited to see what the soldiers would do.

"Poles," the president called as he came out the door. *"You'll be paid the money you have coming. We don't want any bloodshed. Settle down and wait quietly, or the soldiers will attack."*

We waited that whole afternoon. The hundred strikers stared at the hundred soldiers. I could tell that the men were figuring their chances against the rifles. Tata made me stand behind him. Tempers rose, and men yelled at the soldiers. But it would have been rocks against rifles, and a fight did not break out.

Finally, at five o'clock, the paymaster brought out the men's pay. Then we boarded the train to go back to Buffalo.

As the train swayed on the tracks, Tata put his arm on the seat behind me. "Some things are more important than hard work," he said. "Like today."

He pulled a nickel from his pocket. "This is for you, Stefan. You've been working hard. Buy something for yourself."

"Thank you, Tata," I said, closing my fist on the coin. I would buy some drawing paper. Suddenly, being an artist was important to me again. More important than hard work. I wanted to draw the strikers and the soldiers as they had faced each other that afternoon.

V

FATHER PITASS

Our Polish newspaper supported the strike. Tata stayed with the strikers for a few more days, then turned his mind once again to finding work. Fabianna found a job in the farm fields south of Buffalo. Each day, she walked to the fields with other girls and women. She earned fifteen cents a day.

As I ran errands and did small jobs, I thought of the fine, white drawing paper waiting for me at home. I had tried to draw the strikers one night. The result was that I spoiled a good piece of paper. I wasn't very good at drawing people. Also, Tata got angry with me. He thought drawing was a waste of time. Now the paper was just sitting on the shelf.

One day, I was lucky enough to earn sixteen cents by noon. I decided to take the afternoon off. Mamusia was hanging the wash in the back yard when I came home. The little ones were playing in the grass. I slipped into the kitchen and took my drawing paper. Today I would draw what I was good at.

I decided to draw St. Stanislaus church. It was the most beautiful building I knew. Sitting at the curb across from the church, I got out the paper and my lead pencil. Horses and carts passed by on the busy street as I hunched over and started the sketch. I quickly lost myself in my work. Later, a shadow fell across my paper, and I looked up. It was Father Pitass, my priest.

"A very good sketch," he said. "The windows, stonework, steeple, and stairs. Very good."

I smiled. "Do you really think so, Father?"

"Indeed I do." He rubbed his chin. "Would you sell it to me?"

"Oh, no, Father," I said. "I wouldn't sell a drawing to the church. I would give it. But it should be finished in ink." Of course, I didn't have a pen and ink. What should I do?

It seemed as if Father Pitass could read my mind. "I have ink at the rectory. Come in with me." He helped me to my feet. "You can finish the drawing at my desk."

That's how I ended up sitting at the priest's desk. He paced back and forth across the room as I inked in the sketch. When I finished, I handed him the drawing of the church.

"For you, Father," I said.

"Very nice. Now, perhaps we should take a walk to the carpenter's shop," he said. "He can fix us a frame."

As we were leaving his office, Father Pitass turned and went back to his desk. He picked up the pen and the little bottle of ink. "Never did like this pen," he mumbled. "Here, Stefan, can you take this old pen and ink off my hands?"

I nodded and tucked the pen and small bottle into my pocket. "I think so, Father." I smiled. "Thank you." He winked at me.

At the carpenter shop, the priest looked through the wood scraps until he found some nice pieces. Mr. Bartosiak, the carpenter, cut one piece for backing and glued the drawing in place. Then he made a frame to lay over it. The edges of the frame had a fancy, round cut. It was fine work. He charged Father Pitass twenty cents for the wood and work.

"It looks so good," I said. "Like a real artist's drawing."

Father laughed. "Of course it does." He pulled me along with him down the street. "Let me give you some business advice."

"Business?" I asked. "What do you mean?"

"You have to earn money, and you draw like an angel," he said, gesturing. "Why not do both? I know some shopkeepers who would be proud to have a drawing of their shops."

"They would pay for drawings?"

"Of course. But not too much. Let me think." He stepped off the curb, and we hurried across the street. "You have to pay the carpenter twenty cents. More paper, more ink, glue. Hmmmmm."

The more he thought, the faster Father Pitass walked. I skipped to keep up with him.

"Here it is," he said finally. "I'll be your first customer. You can draw the school. I'll pay you fifty cents for a framed, finished drawing. That should be enough to buy drawing supplies and frames for your next customers."

My head was spinning. Next customers?

"The shopkeepers may not be able to pay as much. Maybe forty cents," he said. "You'll have to try it and see. Now I must rush." He tucked the church drawing under his arm and hurried on his way. I was dismissed. Whew!

The next day, I arrived at the school to draw. I hadn't told anyone at home what I was doing. After inking the drawing, I went to Father Pitass.

"Father," I said, "I have no money for the frame."

He dug around in his pockets for two dimes. "This is called an advance," he said, giving me the coins. "I can trust you not to leave town with my money?"

"Oh, yes," I said, startled. Then I saw he was teasing me.

When the frame was finished, I brought the drawing back to him. Counting out the remaining money he owed into my hand, he said, "It's nice doing business with you."

So, I was in business. I went back to Mr. Bartosiak, the carpenter, and bought another frame. Then I bought glue. I sat at the curb and laid out the supplies from my cloth sack. A frame, drawing paper, pencil, pen and ink, glue. Tomorrow I would look for my next customer. That night I dropped many coins in the money jar.

"A good day, Stefan?" Tata asked me. I did not tell him how I'd earned the money.

The next day I tried at Wozniak's bakery. "Would you buy a drawing of your bakery?" I asked in a rush. "I'll put it in a handsome frame."

Wozniak put his floury hands on his hips. "I would like a

drawing, but how do I know you can draw?" he asked.

"Uh." I hadn't thought of this. "Well . . ." What should I say, I wondered. I decided to tell the truth. "You don't know if I can draw. So I'll do the drawing, and then you can see."

"I may not buy it," he said. "Not if I don't like it."

"How much would you pay if you like it?" I asked.

He shook his head. "How can you ask that? I haven't seen the drawing yet."

I was learning fast. In order to sell a drawing, I would have to finish and frame it first. And I didn't know how much money I could get. Wozniak may not even want it. Sometimes, you have to take risks, I thought. So I went across the street to get a good view of the bakery.

I had just finished inking Wozniak's sign when he came across the street. He looked at the drawing and nodded his head. Some flour fell on the drawing, and I brushed it off.

"It's not framed yet," I said. "Give me a little more time." I was afraid he wouldn't like it.

"I like it already." He pounded me on the back. "Hurry. I want to show my wife."

When I gave him the framed drawing, Wozniak was pleased. He nailed it to the wall above the bread counter. He had not paid me, and I hated to mention the price. Finally, I cleared my throat and said, "How does fifty cents sound to you?"

"I like the sound of forty cents much better," he said.

"All right," I agreed. Just what Father Pitass thought. As Wozniak handed me the coins, I said, "It's nice doing business with you." He shook my hand!

I ran down the street, shouting, "I did it! I did it!" I was a real artist now. After buying another frame, I would have twenty cents for the family. How I got the money was going to be my secret.

VI

THE HOUSE PAYMENT

I was able to sell a drawing each day for four days in a row. But today had been terrible. I had drawn a grocery a few blocks away, and the owner wouldn't buy the drawing. I had nothing to show for the day's work.

Tata was home when I arrived. Mamusia had the money jar on the table. The coins were counted out in stacks.

"We have one more week until the house payment is due," she said. "We may not make it."

Tata was working for the city this week and next week, laying sewer lines. The job would bring in good money while it lasted. But it wasn't enough. He had gone too many days without pay.

"How much did you bring today?" Tata asked us. Fabianna put her fifteen cents on the table. Leon pulled out six cents he had earned at the market. "Stefan?" Tata looked at me.

I hung my head. "Nothing."

"Nothing?" Tata shouted at me. He saw my cloth sack and asked, "What is in there?"

I didn't want to tell him. Because I was slow to answer, he grabbed the sack from me and looked inside. He pulled out the framed grocery drawing and threw it across the room. "We may lose the house," he yelled. "And you do this foolishness? Shame on you." He pointed to the bedroom door. "Go to bed."

I took the grocery drawing out of the frame and glued the new drawing in. I got up and crossed the street slowly. Peeking in the window, I could see the store owner arranging some shirts. Do it, I told myself. I took a deep breath and walked in the door.

The owner saw me and rushed over. *"What are you doing in here?"* he shouted. I guess I didn't look like his other customers. He grabbed my ear and started to drag me outside.

"Ouch!" I cried. I held up the framed picture. *"You vant to buy? Please look."*

He let go of my ear and took the picture. *"Did you do this? It's quite good. The frame is nicely done too."*

"Is my drawing," I explained, as I rubbed my ear. *"I pick dis shop because is pretty."* I pointed to the brickwork in the drawing.

"It's a new building," he said. *"I'm pleased that you chose to draw it. How much money do you want?"*

I wanted to say sixty cents. That was much more than the Polish customers had paid. I hesitated.

Before I could speak, he said, *"I won't pay more than one dollar. Not a penny more."*

I felt like giggling. *"Oh, vell,"* I sighed. *"I agree."* I took the silver dollar from him. It felt as heavy as a sack of flour!

"Come back tomorrow," the owner said. *"You can draw the building next door. It belongs to me too."*

"I vill be here," I said.

When I left the store, I thought I would burst. I ran all the way back to the east side before I let out a whoop. As Mr. Bartosiak made me another frame, he told me to sit still. I was jiggling and bothering his work.

That night I put eighty cents in Tata's hand and told him the whole story.

"Father Pitass suggested this?" he asked.

"He said I draw like an angel, Tata."

He put his hands on my shoulders. "You want to draw so much that you disobeyed me?"

"Yes." I was not proud of disobeying him.

"Why?"

"It was for . . . for bread, as you say," I told him. "I wanted to help take care of us. And bring home more money. Then, at Tonawanda, you said some things are more important than hard work. I did hard work, but I wanted to be drawing."

"That is not exactly what I meant," Tata said sternly.

"You also said sometimes we should take risks."

"I did not mean exactly what you did, Stefan."

I hugged him. "I know, but that's how it made sense to me. I'm sorry I didn't do what you told me to, Tata."

Tata let out a big laugh and squeezed me hard. "Well, I'm not sorry at all. If you can bring home this much money, we'll make the house payment," he said. "What do you think of that?"

Zuzanna, who had been watching us carefully, began to dance around us. "Stefan is a good boy again, isn't he, Tata?"

"He is," Tata laughed. "I am so proud of my son, the artist."

That Sunday in church, I thanked God for my good fortune, and I asked that there would be more jobs for my father.

Tadeusz fell asleep in the church pew. Suddenly, he fell off the pew with a thump. Father Pitass jumped up and pointed at me. It wasn't me, I thought. Please don't yell at me.

But his loud voice boomed out, "I will not have any noise in my church. Children must be quiet. Even if they are artists who sell drawings in downtown Buffalo."

My face turned red. Fabianna and Feliks were giggling. Everyone was looking at me. I saw Tata nod his head. I looked up at Father Pitass, who winked. Now, because of what the priest had yelled at me, every shopkeeper in the neighborhood would want a drawing by Stefan Nowicki!

We made the house payment. There was still no meat in the soup, but we had saved the house. Tata found more jobs, because he never stopped trying. I drew shops in the neighborhood and downtown. Fabianna worked hard. Leon and Zuzanna filled the woodshed for next winter. Mamusia managed the money and made sure we made it through the bad times.

Soon, even the bad times passed by.

AMERICA'S PAST

A Powerful Industrial City

By 1893, Buffalo was an important American city. It was a great
inland port and railroad center. Lake
Erie, the Erie Canal, and many railroad lines met here. Goods that came
on ships from the Midwest were transferred to canal barges or trains for
shipment east.

The red line on the map shows
the Erie Canal that connected Buffalo to Albany, New York.

BUFFALO UP TO THE 1890S

In 1813, Buffalo was a small village of five hundred people in
the state of New York. When the British came to burn the village
that year, the people fled. However, the villagers returned a year
later to build again. By 1820, there were two thousand people in
the town.

Buffalo is located at the eastern end of Lake Erie. The town
grew on land that sloped down to the waterfront. By 1825, the Erie
Canal had been dug. It connected Buffalo to Albany on the
Hudson River. Now, goods from Lake Erie could be transferred at
Buffalo to the canal for shipment to the Hudson River and the
ocean. Buffalo became a great inland port city.

Lake ships arrived from Chicago and other ports in the Midwest. Goods such as grain, lumber, hogs and cattle, lead and
copper, and furs flowed into Buffalo on their way east. There were
many jobs at the docks. The workers took goods from the lake

ships and put them on the canal barges.

By the 1850s, many goods were transferred to the growing railroads as well as the canal barges. More jobs were created, and the population of the great city grew. Industries that dealt with goods from the Mid-

The Polish immigrants raised money to build their own churches.

west grew. There were breweries, paper mills, shipyards, slaughterhouses, and iron foundries that made tools and other products.

Immigrants from other countries came to Buffalo to take the jobs. By 1890, when Buffalo had over 250,000 people, three-fourths of them were immigrants. The Irish and the Germans had come first. They established their own neighborhoods. The Poles started coming to Buffalo in large numbers in the 1880s. They settled on Buffalo's east side. Each group, including white and black Americans, made their own neighborhoods.

Cattle from the Midwest were shipped to Buffalo for processing.

Some years were good for the city. Other times were bad, and many people were out of work. However, the hard times did not last long. Business soon improved, and Buffalo was once again a busy, bustling city.